I LIKE VEG!

BROCCOL
DELICILL

ONIONUS
EMOTIONALLUS

This Faber book belongs to

....

BEETROETU
HORRIBLE

KEEP IT GREEN

POTATUS
MASHABLLUS

CARROTUS
SEE IN THE

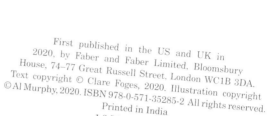

SUN
LIGHT

**For the peas in my pod –
Sean, Teddy and Bobo.
C. F.**

**For Casper. You are
bonkers, and I wouldn't
want it any other way.
A. M.**

AIR

First published in the US and UK in 2020, by Faber and Faber Limited, Bloomsbury House, 74–77 Great Russell Street, London WC1B 3DA. Text copyright © Clare Foges, 2020. Illustration copyright © Al Murphy, 2020. ISBN 978-0-571-35285-2 All rights reserved. Printed in India
1 3 5 7 9 10 8 6 4 2
The moral rights of Clare Foges and Al Murphy have been asserted. A CIP record for this book is available from the British Library.

BUTTER
NUTTY
SQUASH

FABER & FABER

has published children's books since 1929. Some of our very first publications included *Old Possum's Book of Practical Cats* by T. S. Eliot, starring the now world-famous Macavity, and *The Iron Man* by Ted Hughes. Our catalogue at the time said that 'it is by reading such books that children learn the difference between the shoddy and the genuine'. We still believe in the power of reading to transform children's lives.

FUN
FUN
FUN

FESTIVAL

*ACTUALLY
A FRUIT

WATER

VEG PATCH PARTY

CLARE FOGES & AL MURPHY

Every night down on the farm
When Farmer stops for tea,

When all the cows are tucked up tight
And all the pigs asleep...

The vegetables start waking up.
They stretch and rise and shine.

They drag out lots of stages
Cos it's VEGGIE PARTY TIME!

POTATO is the first on stage
With backing band The Chips.
He shouts 'VEGGIES, ARE YOU READDDY!'
Then plays his latest hits.

Next up it's ~~the~~ The Superstar-
The singing, dancing PUMPKIN.

She gets the parsnips jivin'
And she sets the turnips jumpin'.

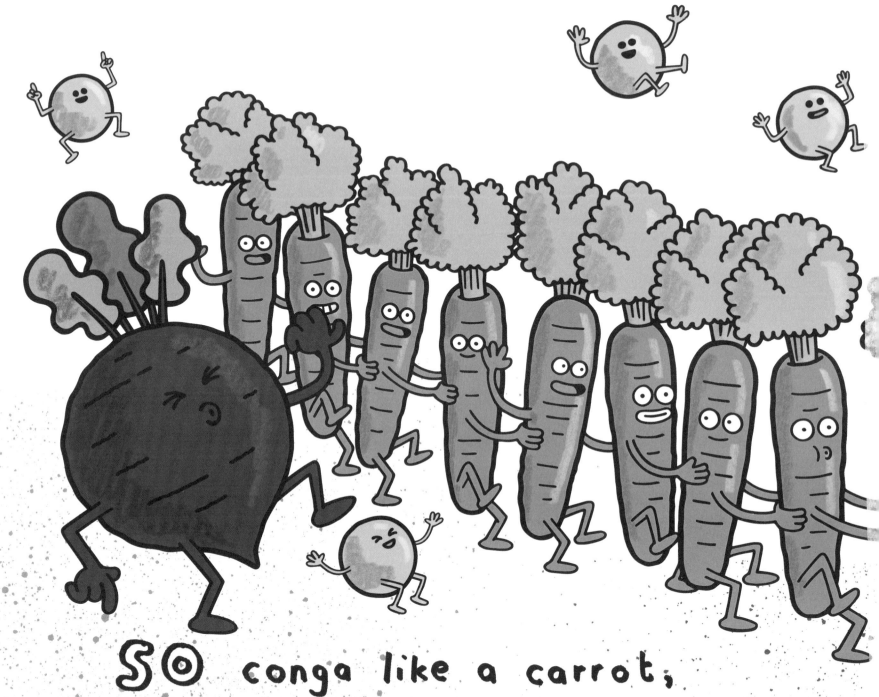

So conga like a carrot,
Party like a pea,
Rock out like a radish, **YEAH!**
And boogie like a bean!

It's called the veg patch party.
It's muddy, loud and fun...
So get your veggie wiggle on
And rock out EVERYONE!

Now...
RED HOT CHILLIS
take the stage —
The coolest band you've seen.
They play their rockin' music
To a crowd of runner beans.

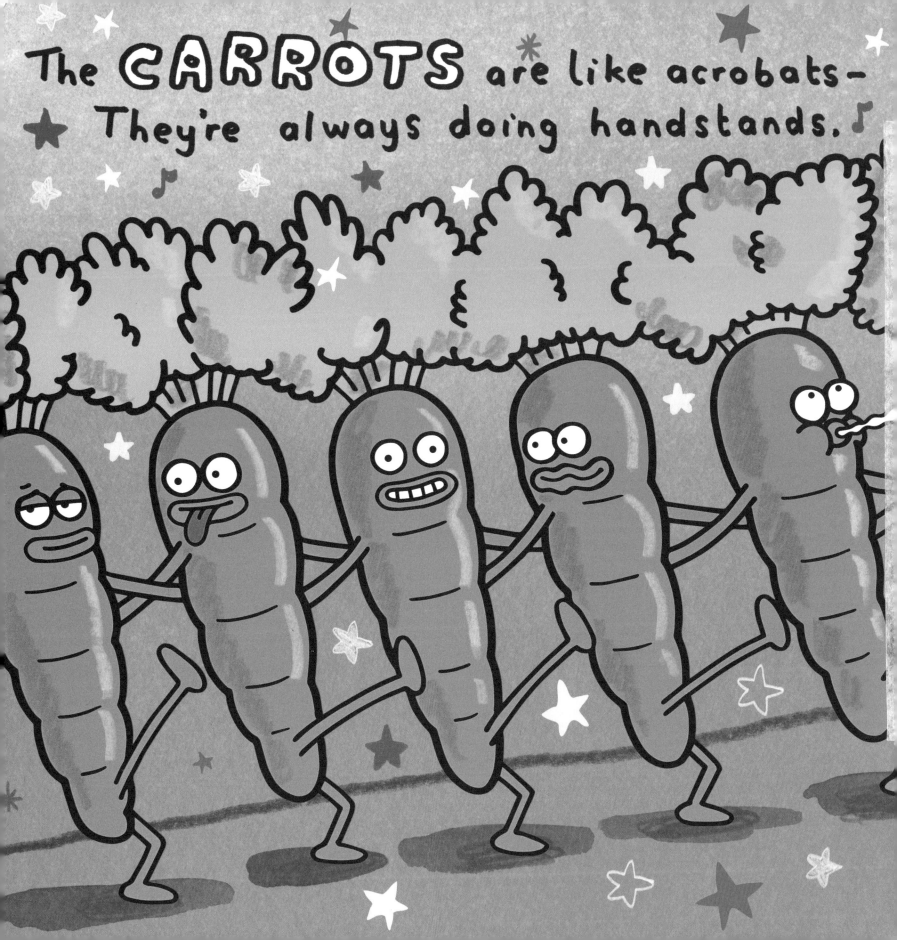

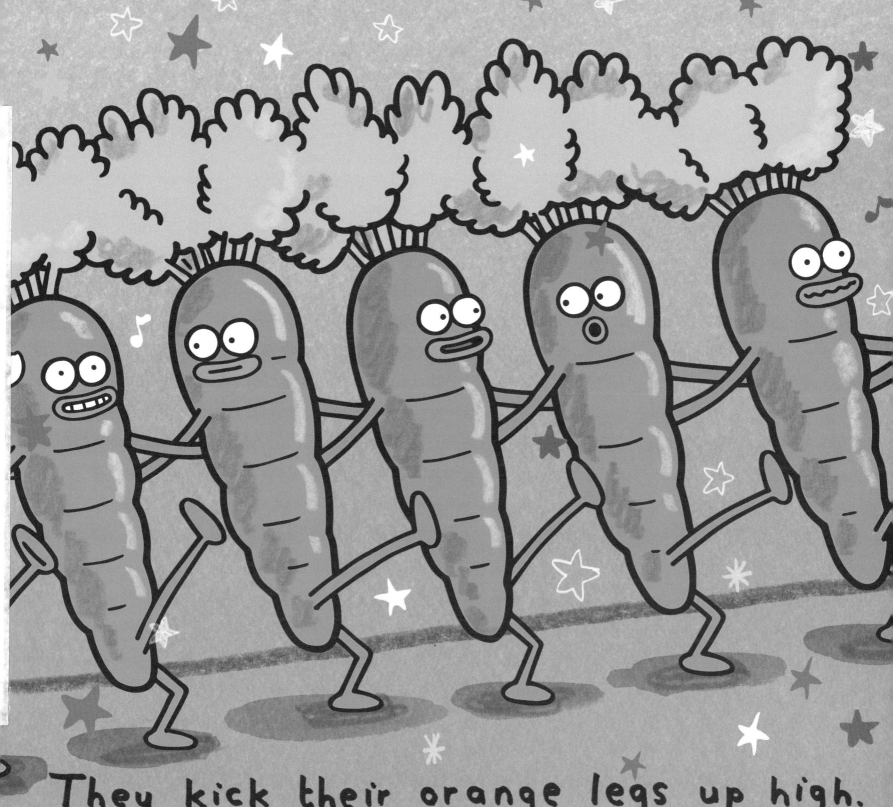

They kick their orange legs up high.
It's called ~~the~~ the **CARROT CAN CAN!**

The **PEAS** get so excited.
They bounce and scream and shout.
Up next on stage it's Techno King —
Yes...

DJ BRUSSEL SPROUT

DJ Brussel spins the decks
The peas bounce high to dance...
With mudballs, lights and veggie beats
He has them in a trance!

SO conga like a carrot,
Party like a pea,
Rock out like a radish, **YEAH!**
And boogie like a bean !

It's called the veg patch party.
It's muddy, loud and fun...
So get your veggie wiggle on
And rock out EVERYONE!

Now **TURNIP** jumps down in the mud,
And pumpkin follows... CRASH!

Next the peas all tumble in.
They skid, they skate, they SPLASH!

Check out those veggies going mad. They're all on stage together!

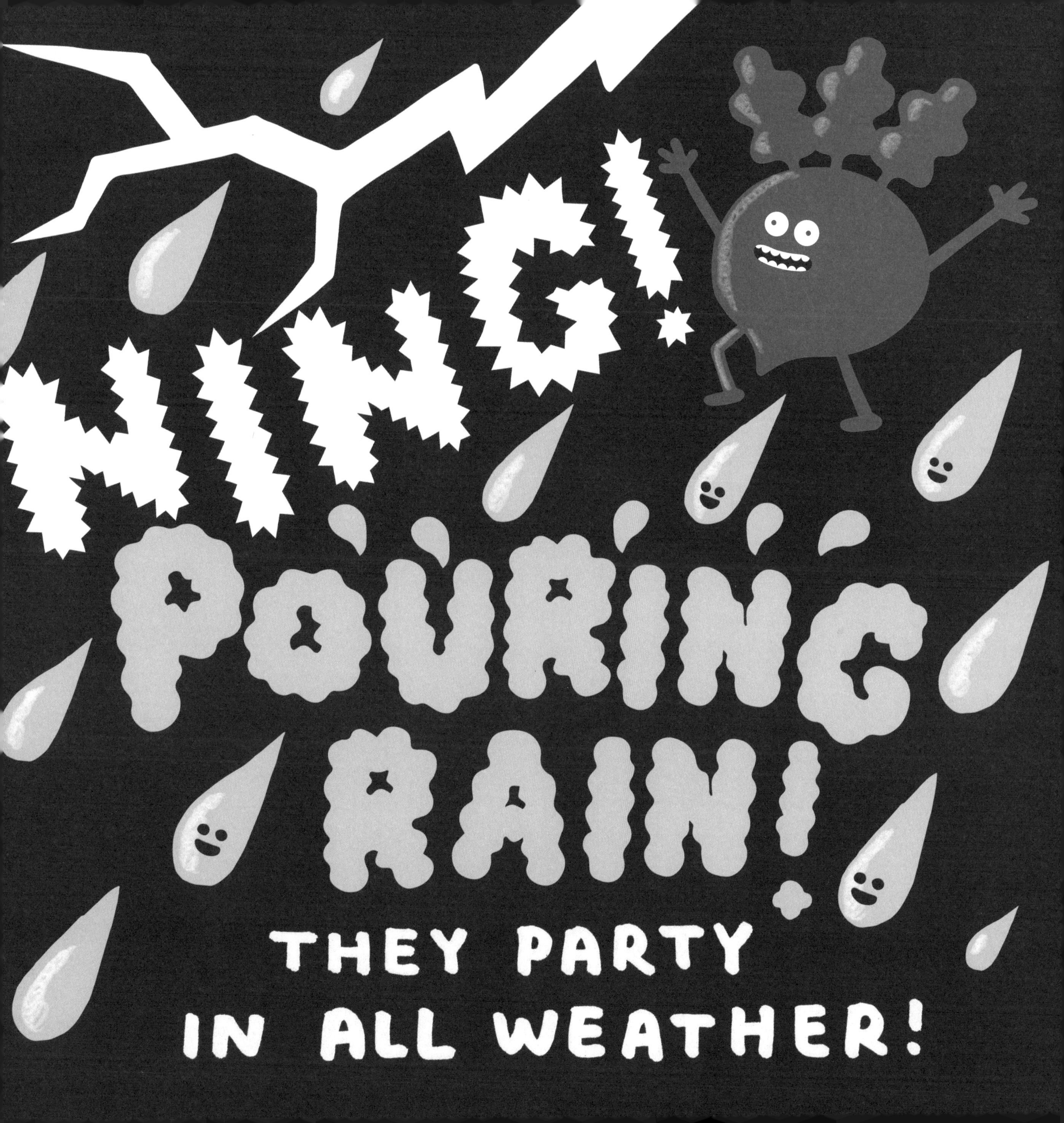
NING!
POURING RAIN!
THEY PARTY
IN ALL WEATHER!

SO conga like a carrot,
Party like a pea,
Rock out like a radish, **YEAH!**
And boogie like a bean!

It's called the veg patch party.
It's muddy, loud and fun...
So get your veggie wiggle on
And rock out EVERYONE!

YES...

So now you know what happens
When the moon is shining white
The veggies have a crazy time
And party through the night!

So conga like a carrot...

I LIKE VEG!

BROCCO[L]
DELICI[OUS]

ONIONUS
EMOTIONALLUS

BIETAROTUS
HORRIBILLUS

KEEP IT GREEN

POTATUS
MASHABLLUS

CARROTU[S]
SEE IN TH[E]